2 AM Running in Fear

by

Barbie K. Lewis and Jasmine N. Lewis

DORRANCE
PUBLISHING CO
EST. 1920
PITTSBURGH, PENNSYLVANIA 15238

Dorrance Publishing Co
585 Alpha Drive
Pittsburgh, PA 15238
Visit our website at *www.dorrancebookstore.com*

ISBN: 978-1-6491-3321-2
eISBN: 978-1-6491-3288-8

It all started at the dinner table. Ray got a phone call from his secretary. I could hear her saying, "I miss you, I can't wait to see you again." When she hung up, I asked Ray why she was saying that to him. Ray looked up at me and said, "What are you talking about now?" I answered, "Ray, I heard what she said."

All at once Ray jumped up from the table, came over to me, pushed me to the floor. Ray fell to his knees, slapped me, and told me he would be better off without me. As he raised his fist to hit me, I covered my face with my arms. Ray pulled my arms, holding my arms with his knees. He began to punch me as hard as he could. I felt the punches over and over.

I was out of breath and bleeding from my nose and mouth. The harder I tried to fight back, the harder his punches would get. His cell phone rang, which stopped his punches. Ray answered the phone as if nothing was happening. It took all my might to get up off the floor.

I made it to the bathroom, cleaned myself up, took a shower, and got on the bed to pray. Soon Ray came to bed. I did not move, I waited for Ray to fall asleep. My chest hurting, and my neck sore. The punches from Ray's heavy hands still made it hard to breathe.

2 AM

Nervously, I eased out of bed, making my way to the front room. I pulled my hidden suitcase and shoes from behind the chair that I placed weeks ago for my escape. I slowly removed the keys from the keyholder, gently opened the door. I did not waste any time to close the door behind me, every second counted. Having a panic attack, I made it to the car, putting the suitcase in front, and drove away.

With fear I continued to look back, hoping he was not behind me. Thirty minutes had passed, and I felt safe enough to slow the car down and drive the given speed.

I did not put a coat on, just left. The snow was falling as I drove, ice still on the car. I did not give the car time to warm up, I just took off. For it to be early morning hours, the car lights shiny on the road made the snow look thick and the sky bright white fog. The further south I got to the Florida line, I would be back in warmer weather again.

Ray did not turn abusive until he started his new job as CEO of the Power Company. Ray would always work late hours and had grown less interest in me. Most nights Ray's temper flared up at the kitchen table after his conversations on the phone. I never could find out who or what the calls were about. It never failed, every night he always used my body for releasing his stress, whether it be physical, mental, or sexual.

A New Start

8 AM

Still shaken up from my morning, I made it to the Georgia airport. I parked the car to make it seem I had taken a flight. I loaded my face with makeup to cover all my red spots. I took a cab to the local bus station, purchased a ticket to South Alabama. The bus ride calmed my nerves, the snow was no more, it was now fall again, which was enough for a nap and to look at my paperwork.

I had been smart to open a savings account without Ray knowing. I purchased a car and a small home off the internet. For two years, I had been working on this plan and it had finally paid off. I found a good deal on the Alabama-Florida line in a small town in Alabama called Sharp, paid it in full. For so long I was afraid to leave, not sure I could make it on my own. I got tired of the constant abuse. I was getting suicidal and having to see a psychiatrist.

12 PM

I arrived in Sharp Town, Alabama. I collected my belongings and called the car dealership from the bus station, bought a cell phone from the market store across the street. The car dealership was a block away. I was proud to walk and pick up my car. The car lot was not busy, I was able to finalize my paperwork and be on my way. Next, I drove to the realtor, there was more paperwork involved at this stop.

Soon I could sign and get my keys to my new home. The realtor wanted to give me a tour of my new home and neighborhood, I refused. She told me the property had been vacant for two years and needed some yardwork. There was no need for a tour, I was ready to start my new life.

As I drove, I noticed my home is thirty minutes from the city, which put a big smile on my face. On my way, I saw a small market. I stopped to pick up a few items to get me settled in. I had to get some alcohol to soak my aching body in. Following my directions, I was led to a dirt road that only had five homes with a large field in the middle.

The fourth home was my new haven. As I got closer, I noticed there were items at my door entrance. Not knowing what to expect, I took the keys to my home and went to the door. A big note on the door: "Welcome to the neighborhood, Rebecca." A nice basket of fruit from Bill and Gladys, fresh baked goods from Paul and Linda, vegetables from Floyd and Wendy, and flowers from William and Peggy. And to top that, a note that read: "Welcome to the family, come to the playground tomorrow at noon for meet-and-greet." The realtor must have informed them that I would be coming. I felt very welcomed.

I opened the door, placed all the items my new neighbors had left for me on the table. The home was so cozy inside, the previous owners sold me the home fully furnished, which made me more thankful. I unloaded the car with my belongings, the fresh air and the comfort of the new place took tension off me. I returned inside, walked around my two-bedroom, two-bath home. I had enough room to make a small office and den. I put all belongings in order, took a pain pill, soaked in my hot alcohol bath, and got into bed.

2 AM

I woke from sleep in terror. I dreamed I never made it to the car. Ray had pulled me by the hair, dragged me back into the house with my feet scraping the porch. As Ray raised his hand to hit me, I sat up in bed with a scream. It took me a while to calm myself down and think, I did make it. "I'm okay now, I'm okay now," I said, over and over. Placing my mind on my new home and the lovely gifts my neighbors had given me eased me back to sleep.

The bright light from the morning sky awakened me. I went to the kitchen, turned on the coffee pot, and made toast. I finished my coffee at the desk, called my attorney, gave him my new number and address where he could reach me when my divorce papers were final. On my computer, I searched for local thrift stores and shopping areas, one of my escapes from everyday life is window shopping. I needed more clothes and shoes and personal items that I left behind, so maybe I would do more than window shop.

It was almost noon. I needed to freshen up for the neighbors' meet-and-greet. I always said a little prayer before gatherings and anything that I did. Ray said I was stupid when it came to anything but housework. If I was submissive in his world of living, he was pleased with me. "So, Lord, I ask that you talk for me, keep me silent when needed to be."

As I made my way to the playground, I could feel my anxiety starting. I took a deep breath, counted to ten, and thought of positive thoughts to keep me relaxed. A lady sat, watching me approach, and introduced herself as Gladys. She told me all about the other neighbors and which homes they lived in. Gladys' husband, Bill, had a garden in their backyard and offered me to come over anytime for fresh fruit.

Then Paul and Linda walked over with smiles of joy on their faces, their smiles put a little joy in me. Paul and Linda owned the local baker's shop and gave me a gift card to the store. Floyd and Wendy, carrying lemonade and ice, told me all about their vegetable garden and I was welcome to vegetables anytime. Last, William and Peggy, owners of the local flower store, gave me seeds and bulbs to put in my planters.

Each couple made me feel at home, which helped me with conversation. For once I was me and was proud, I could speak without fear. The day was perfect, we ladies laughed and talked while the men grilled. Gladys invited me to walk with her to her home to get the slaw, baked beans, and corn for the meal. As we walked, she pointed to the woods in the back of the homes and demonstration how pretty it looked in the fall.

After we had lunch, they all exchanged numbers with me and we returned to our homes. I got to my front porch, sat down in the rocker chair to view each couple's home and learn my surroundings, which put security in my heart. The view from my home, the pavilion is in the middle of the homes, a pretty sight it is. Beautiful flowers were growing on both sides of the pavilion and a small playground to the left, a tennis court and basketball court on the right. All the viewing made me get up with excitement to plant my seeds and bulbs in my planters.

I rushed to the small shed on the side of the house to see if I had any tools. I opened the door and smiled. I was so thankful and grateful of the previous owners. They left everything, God blessed them with a small fortune up North and I was blessed in return. "God is Good." I planted dwarf ranunculus in the small planters on both side of the steps.

The coleus in the flowerbeds on both sides of the walkway and to line the front of the house. My last flower marigold I put in the planter by the mailbox. Now I would be able to enjoy my home even more. I put my gardening tools away and watered all the seeds and bulbs. One last look. Yes, perfect it will be.

5 PM

Before I knew it, time had passed me by. I got my bathwater ready while I made coffee to relax after my hot bath. My bath was very relaxing, I got my coffee and went to the living room to my recliner. Not a light on in the house. The only noise that could be heard was the sound of the wall clock, as the second hand moved. Holding a cup of coffee in my right hand, feeling the heat from the cup massage my fingers.

6 PM

I got up to open the window to be at peace with the coolness of the evening air as it flowed through the house. Hard to believe it was the last week in August. As the sky got darker, the shadows of the trees and mountains moved with the setting of the sun. The sound of the beetles, crickets, grasshoppers, and cicadas brought the night in with its special song. The water sprinkler from the neighbor's garden put the icing on the cake. I dosed off to sleep, still holding my cup of coffee. As I fell into deeper sleep, I felt my body relaxing. The wind and the sound of the crickets pampered me like a music box playing softly in my ears.

2 AM

During my peaceful sleep, I was awakened by a loud, terrifying noise. My cup of coffee hit the floor. The sound was like an explosion nearby. It took me a minute to move, I wasn't sure if I was dreaming. I grabbed my flashlight, I got up to check the house.

I knew my way around the house, so I did not turn on any lights, the noise sounded as if it came from outside. I looked out each window, I found nothing, not a sign that could have made the noise. None of my neighbors seemed to have heard the noise because there was no movement at their homes. The rest of my night was restless. Trying to take my mind off the noise, I thought about all my plans, about what I would like to do with my new life. Soon I was asleep.

Before long, it was daylight, felt as if I had been sleeping for five minutes. I wasted no time to go outside and check around, still nothing was found or to be seen that would explain the noise. Come to think of it, once before I was snoring in my sleep and scared myself awake. Just maybe that was what happened. I went back into the house, got into the shower, fixed my breakfast, and put my jogging suit on for my morning walk.

Ray thinks I am from Georgia. After my grandmother passed, my mom moved to Georgia and I finished high school there. My roots are here in Alabama. I bet he was in Georgia now looking for me. Well, the joke is on you now, baby.

My morning walks reminded me why I moved out here. I was born and raised in the city. The clutter of people, buildings, cars, and noise I hated. When I would visit my grandparents on the weekend in the country, I loved it. Homes in the country are minutes apart, not ten steps away.

You can have your animals, no chaos, a little freedom. Most of all, you are not watching your back with others in your business. TV and internet have bad service out here, phone service is so-so. We had no city water; our water came from the springs in the cave. Most of the city people came out to the cave with gallon jugs for the fresh spring water. I do say, the spring water was very refreshing. The four families paid the city to run power and gas lines to our homes.

When Ray and I got married we bought property in Tennessee, near his family. My doctor put me on disability due to a chemical spill at the plant where I worked. The chemicals did damage to some of my organs, and a case of asthma. The chemical spill did me no good mentally. I had a rough childhood, a bad marriage, along with friends that I let take advantage of me. Some say I'm too easygoing, others say I put my heart in everything. Or they say I'm too giving. And the two that get under my skin is when they say, "Stop trying to save everybody, and why are you trying to get praises?" I was always taught to do unto others as you would have them do unto you.

I think it's more mean-hearted people in the world than good. The bad thing about it, I have tried to be a mean, it just did not work. I would feel bad about what I'd done and my conscience got the best of me. The only relief I got was to go back and fix it. Love has always been in my heart for others. Even the worst of us have some good in us.

Beloved, if God so loved us, we also ought to love one another. My grandmother made me remember these Bible verses: 1 Peter 3:8-12 KJV: "Finally, be ye all of one mind, having compassion one of another; love as brethren, be pitiful, be courteous; not rendering evil for evil, or railing for railing; but contrariwise blessing; knowing that ye are thereunto called, that ye should inherit a blessing. For he that will love life, and see good days, let him refrain his tongue from evil, and his lips that they speak no guile. Let him turn eschew evil, and do good; let him seek peace, and ensue it. For the eyes of the Lord are over the righteous, and his ears are open unto their prayers; but the face of the Lord is against them that do evil," along with Mark 12:30-31.

I didn't like living and being alone, but it was better than having someone hitting you, fussing at you, and complaining about everything you did. Just to think about Ray put chills on my body. I tried so hard to please Ray but each time didn't even matter. I would work so hard at making him happy, in the end I would lose each time. No matter how hard I tried, it was always wrong. I was free now to be myself. I could laugh and cry without being ashamed.

I used to be afraid that my laughter was at the wrong thing or the wrong time. Now I could cry without being judged and discouraged. No more fears that my cry was not worth a tear. Now I laughed and cried out loud just for the hell of it. I could now talk to others without getting an okay to speak. I could now laugh at jokes and express my own opinion without holding my head down.

7:30 AM

Enough about the past, time to get back home, freshen up, and head into town. The walk back was shorter. I noticed I had only walked one mile, I had to do better. A few items to pick up at the market, the library for internet surfing, and lunch at the library grill. For a Saturday morning, the library would not be crowded with students, which made it easier to get a computer.

Even though I got the local newspaper, the library computer provided me with world news also. As I walked out my door, I heard voices. I noticed my neighbor Bill with blueprints in his hand, he was having workers working out in the field. Different types of tractors and trucks in the middle of the field. I asked Bill what was going on, he said, "We are making a small lake for all to enjoy."

I was so excited to hear the good news. They had been planning this for a year, now plans for them were turning visible. The lake would be in the huge field in the center of all five houses. It might take each family five minutes to get there but it would be well worth it. I said my goodbyes to Bill, got my notebook and pen, on my way to the library. When I pulled up at the library, I went straight over to the grill, ordered me a grilled chicken sandwich to go. As I waited on my order, I looked around at the sections of the library I wanted to explore. Soon my order was up, before I walked out, I stopped by the main desk and got a library card and membership for the bookstore.

I walked outside, rushed to my car, got in, and like always the traffic and noise in the city made me nervous. People yelling and horns blowing. Everything was just too close, like it was all closing in on me. I drove a little faster before I had a panic attack. I did not want to see another psychiatrist for any reason at all. I've had my share of that with my childhood, marriage, and the chemical deal at work.

At the edge of town there was a small market store, I stopped to get a few items for the house. When I opened the car door there was a family in a car next to mine. Looked to be husband, wife, and small child, around six years old, in the back seat. The man was saying the most hurtful things to this woman, I wanted to cry. I had to stuff my feelings in my gut and get in the store and hope they would be gone when I returned to my car. Inside the sound of jazz music took my mind off the man outside, and when I saw my double chocolate fudge cake I was in heaven.

Making my way to the checkout, with my loaf of bread, tuna, fruit, and my double chocolate fudge cake. Not paying attention to what I was doing, I ran my buggy right into the man in front of me. I apologized for my clumsiness, he gave me his forgiveness. As we waited in line, he turned to me and introduced himself. Told me his name was Sam, I told him mine was Rebecca and it was nice to meet him. I had to think quick, so I said, "I just remembered, I forgot my eggs," and I rushed away. Did not want to stir up nothing, things were going too well for me now to mess up with some man.

3 PM

I waited till I saw Sam check out and go to his car and leave before I went back to the checkout line. When I got to my car, I turned on my radio so I could enjoy my ride home. Finally, I was on the dirt road that led home. Once I hit the dirt road, it was like I had crossed over into another world. I was safe again from all my anxieties.

I pulled up to my home, parked the car, rolled down my window, and just looked at my wonderful home I had been blessed with. The air was different from the city air, much cleaner smell. The sound of nature to my ears, not chaos of man. As I opened my car door, I noticed two squirrels playing near the bird feeder, and eating the seeds that the birds had dropped. You can't find this freedom in the big city. Just looked at them enjoying God's grace.

Not wanting to rush the squirrels away, I did a little cleaning inside the car. During my cleaning, I looked over bulletins from churches I had collected from the library. The free cookbook with my favorite meals and cooking tips. Found a pair of earrings I lost when I was unpacking the car. And lucky me, a twenty-dollar bill under the seat. I went to the other side of the car to see if I had any treasures there, all I found was a cookie that looked like it had been there before I purchased the car.

I stuffed all my bulletins and reading material in my bag, got my groceries, and went into my house. I went to the kitchen table, put all I had in my arms on the table. Took my clothes off, got into the shower, put my pajamas on. Living alone with no one to answer to is no limits on what time to have pajamas on. I took my teakettle, added water, turned the eye of the stove on, reached for a cup and a teabag, placed it on the counter.

While waiting on my water to heat, I got all my material I had collected from the car and took them to the patio. From my patio, I could see the markings in the field, which would be the lake soon. There went the sound of my teakettle, as I poured the water in my teacup, the smell eased the tension of the day. Sorting through all my material, I caught up on all my Bible reading, sorted events that were upcoming, and added them on my calendar. Having my calendar full of activities helps when I get bored and feel lonely.

I did find something in my material that caught my attention, a family in the city needing a sitter for their elderly mother. During high school and college, I was a certified nurse assistant, enjoyed providing care in the local nursing home and providing care for local families. Thought I would give them a call. I dialed the number, it took six rings before anyone answered, I almost hung up till a voice on the other end said, "Sims residence, Jeff, may I help you?" I stated my name and told the man I was inquiring about the ad for sitter. Jeff said, "Thank you, can you be here next Friday morning at 9:30 am sharp for an interview?" I told him yes, he gave me the address and said, "See you then."

5 PM

I finished my calendar, looked like September would fly by if I kept myself active (church, Bible study, library, crafts, local events, and voluntary work). All looked overwhelming, but I would have satisfaction in my choices. I needed to get up and fix my dinner. A quick pasta salad would do with a glass of wine. A little wine helped me sleep at night. I had trouble at night breathing, sometimes I woke myself up, out of breath due to my asthma. And the next morning, tired and with a headache. Doctors say I do not have sleep apnea, so I treat myself. Along with the wine, I made a pillow wedge to keep my head elevated and my inhaler on my nightstand. After dinner, I did a few squats, took my shower, and got into bed. I refused to fall asleep in the recliner tonight.

Before going to sleep, I always say my prayers and talk to God. I can talk to Him for hours. "God, I am lonely but when I was married, I was not able to talk out loud to you without being laughed at." Another reason why I was happy to be alone and far away, others might think I was going crazy for talking to myself. I went to sleep thinking about my plans for tomorrow.

2 AM

I was awakened by the ringing of my cell phone. Who was calling at this time of morning, had to be the wrong number. I answered the phone. The voice on the other end said, "You can't run!" I dropped the phone on the floor. My heart racing, I lost my breath, grabbed my inhaler, and tried to remember, was that the voice of Ray? There was no way that Ray knew where I was. I used my address in Georgia for my divorce. I looked at the phone to see the number and name, it had no call. The last call to me was the realtor. And the last call I made was to the Sims.

5 AM

I was unable to go back to sleep, so I went to the kitchen, organized the food closet. Not much in my food closet, I made labels for my storage containers. When I pulled out the washer and dryer to sweep, I noticed a small door. I opened the little door and of course it was dark. I went to my shelf and got my flashlight.

I had to get on my hands and knees to see in. I noticed a light switch. I pulled it, to my surprise the light came on. The little area was empty and very clean. I wondered what in the world it was used for. The area was only big enough to crawl around in, so I knew I would not be using it. I turned the light off and placed the washer and dryer back in place.

After my early morning wakeup experience, I thought I would make an appointment with a psychiatrist later today. I was tired of the 2 am wakeups. I had not been on my medication since the day I left Ray. Maybe that was my problem. I fixed my morning coffee, opened the bay window, and noticed how pretty the sun was coming up.

This was a good time to water all my plants and sweep my porch. It was still early enough to paint my birdbath and the statue of the little girl with a bird in her hand. I found a gallon of white unopened paint and began to paint. I stood back to look at my work and I was very satisfied with what I had done. It felt good knowing I could do something right and make something look pretty.

8 AM

I went back inside, got my local directory off my desk to look up the number for a psychiatrist. There were two in the area, I chose the female psychiatrist. I just didn't want a male for my psychiatrist right now. The reason for the need of a psychiatrist was due to a male. I did not want to be judgmental to my psychiatrist. On the first ring I was able to make an appointment and to my surprise I could go today. I hung up the phone, changed clothes, made a list of all the medications I used to be on, and headed to the car.

I finally made it to my appointment. For some reason it took me forever to get there. I had plenty of energy due to the lack of sleep I had. I walked in, signed my name and had a seat, pulled out my notebook to make notes to tell her. If I didn't make notes, I would forget to tell her the most important things that were happening to me, and that had happened to me. I looked up from my notes and saw a few people of all ages. I wondered if they had experienced some of the things in life as I had.

My name was called to go to room 5. I walked in and I was amazed at the room. Not what I was used to. There was a sofa, recliner, snacks, fish tank, and a desk, which the psychiatrist sat at and took notes. Not just an office with two chairs and a desk.

I stood, not sure what to do. Soon the door opened, and my psychiatrist introduced herself as Mrs. Waters. Mrs. Waters told me to have a seat and make myself comfortable. First question I was asked, had I seen a psychiatrist before? I took a deep breath, told her yes. Question after question I told my stories, about the chemical accident on the job. The relationship with my soon-to-be ex-husband, Ray, and my childhood life.

I was also asked about medications I was on and what did I get diagnosed with. I gave her my list of medications and told her I was diagnosed with bipolar schizophrenia. I explained the medication helped at one time. Dealing with Ray and everyday life put a toll on me. When the medications quit working, I began to feel guilty, sad, unworthy, and just wanted it all to end.

I explained I didn't get much sleep because of my moods. Sometimes I would have so much energy and other times I just stayed in bed. When I found out the truth about Ray and the other women, that was when the medication no longer worked. Ray was no longer a part of my life, I didn't understand why I was still feeing all these things. Then I told Mrs. Waters about my 2 am wakeup stories.

Mrs. Waters did not talk much, only took notes. Mrs. Waters gave me new medications and a card with my next appointment. She did say I should feel better once the medication got in my system. After my session with Mrs. Waters, her assistant gave me a brochure on meetings and group session times, I was ready to start living a normal life and enjoy others as well.

On my way home I stopped by the pharmacies to pick up my medications. The mall was near, I just had to go in to find a nice outfit to wear for my interview tomorrow. I love working with the elderly and disabled, they are appreciative. This job would help me get back on track mentally. After shopping I stopped by Paw Paw's Hamburgers, was told the hamburgers were great and freshly made as you ordered.

As I waited for my burger, I focused on the view of the city. Looking at the city from a distance was not so bad, not so stressful. Everyone was doing their everyday thing and it looked at peace from here. Funny to say once I got down in the city it was a different story. Everyone was rushing, no peace and plenty of chaos.

I jumped as my number was called over the intercom. The loudness of the intercom broke my daydreaming with a laugh. Driving home was different this time, having to tell Mrs. Waters all about my past made me a little depressed. I could not focus on the new me for replaying different parts of my past in my mind.

As I pulled into my neighborhood, I saw Linda walking to her mailbox. She saw me coming, I rolled down my window to speak. "Hi, Linda, how was your day at the bakery?"

"Hi, Rebecca, my day was great, I have some pastries I brought home and I would like to share with you. It will keep me and Paul from eating them all."

"Thank you, Linda, I would love to have them."

Linda rushed into her home, returned with a bag of goodies. "Rebecca, I hope you enjoy."

"Linda, I will, the pastries will come in handy with my tea and coffee, thank you again and enjoy the rest of your evening."

Seeing Linda took my mind off my sadness. I was so thankful I was here with good neighbors and could snap back into joy quickly now.

When I got home, I could not wait to put a pot of coffee on and taste one of Linda's goodies. I took a shower while the coffee was being made, put on my long pink cotton gown that reminded me of my mother when I would go visit her on Saturdays. When Mother retired, she started enjoying her life with the seniors and church group and always had a smile on her face. Something I never did see as a child, my mother smiling. I kept all my problems to myself, I didn't want her to worry, it was time for her to live her life without stress.

Coffee was ready, grabbed a goody and headed to my recliner. Linda's baked goods were always so moist, it was like getting a hug. As I ate and sipped on my coffee, I watched the wind lightly blowing through the trees. As the evening got darker and darker, I didn't budge to move from my recliner. I pulled the blanket that was folded from the couch over me and off to sleep I went.

The Footsteps

2 AM

A noise from the kitchen, I opened my eyes to listen again. It sounded like soft footsteps across the kitchen floor. I rose slowly up out of bed. As I got out of bed the storage door opened and closed. I made it to the kitchen, turned the light on quickly, no one or nothing was there. I went to the back door to check, it was locked and secured.

I just didn't understand, I should have started my medications last night. I poured water into a glass, stood in the kitchen for fifteen minutes, wondering if I was having a nervous breakdown. Every morning at 2 A.M., all this must be in my head. No, I would not claim that. I went to my recliner, got my Bible, and studied till I was asleep.

7 AM

The brightness of the sky from the bay window woke me with its pleasant good morning. I got up, grabbed my medications. I placed the container by my coffee machine to make sure I would not forget a dosage. I couldn't afford to miss. I must get my mental problem back online.

I needed to do something active today with others. After I took my medication, I put a pair of old blue jeans on and a t-shirt. Found some old shoes I did not mind getting dirty, grabbed my keys, I walked over to Floyd and Wendy's home. When I got to their home Wendy and Floyd were in the greenhouse, tending to the vegetable garden. I knocked on the door.

Wendy came to the door with a big smile. "Come in, Ms. Rebecca, you are just in time to help pick tomatoes. Floyd and I have enough to make a vegetable basket for each family, with your help we can get it done by noon."

I put a pair of gloves on, got on my knees and helped. As we worked Wendy talked about her plans with the vegetable store and how she wanted to expand the greenhouse. Talking with Wendy helped me so much.

I learned a lot about vegetable growing and how to store them. I had to laugh at Floyd, he mostly sat back and dosed off as we worked. We finished the baskets, loaded up two wheelbarrows, and carried to each family in the neighborhood. We did not knock, just left the baskets on the front door. Wendy was right, all the baskets were done and delivered by noon.

We returned to Wendy's home; Floyd had made us a bacon tomato sandwich with tea. I sat on the back porch with them as we talked, I viewed the large vegetable field and the greenhouse. The field was shaped like a puzzle and perfect. I noticed how lovely Floyd treated Wendy and how he took his time to understand her as she talked about her plans. I noticed how Wendy took care of Floyd and he was pleased. Their love made me feel happy. It made me feel at peace that Wendy was happy and okay in her marriage.

I hated to leave, but I needed to get home and make my own plans. Start on my everyday activities to keep me active. After my shower I went to my desk, made a to-do list for each day of the week. I would go sign up for a gym membership today. Figured if I wore myself out during the day I could sleep and not be bothered by the 2 am wakeups.

I typed the address to the gym in my phone and headed to town. The gym was busy, but I didn't let that stop me. Along with my new membership, I was given a t-shirt and a tour of the gym and how to use the equipment and a website to visit if I forgot how to use the equipment. I purchased a locker to put items in and got a schedule of the different classes they offered. The gym had its own store, but kind of expensive for me.

I left the gym, stopped by the super store, got me two work outfits for the gym. Went to the gas station, filled my tank up, got me a chicken salad from the deli inside, and went home. It had been a long, good day; I got a little accomplished for myself today. I sat down to eat my salad; the mailman blew his horn to let me know I had mail. I could not wait to get my mail, I ordered a few magazines for entertainment.

I finished my salad, took my evening medications, sorted my magazines to look at and read. I was getting tired and weak. The more I read, the more I got sleepy. I went to the bedroom, pulled my clothes off, naked I laid across my bed. I remembered the evening medication would relax me more and make me sleepy. I laid on the bed, all I could do was look at the ceiling, watching the room get darker and darker.

2 AM

I am awakened by the same noise from the previous night. Okay, this time I knew I was not dreaming, no way! The noise continued this night for ten minutes. As it got softer, I grabbed my house coat, I followed and listened. The noise was coming from my storage room. Terrified, I coached myself in, thinking maybe a squirrel had come in and knocked down a box of cereal. My body shaking as I opened the door, nothing was there, nothing and the noise was gone. Maybe the squirrel was in the loft playing with an acorn, and I scared it away. I checked to see if the back door was locked, once again it was. I returned to bed, listening for the noise and repeating Psalm 23:4-5, 2 Timothy 1:7 the rest of the morning.

9 AM

I decided to get up and take a shower. I was taking a chance on going to the local Catholic church this Sunday morning. A couple invited me to come months ago, so today I would be there for Mass. I belong to a Baptist church, but I have studied the Catholic religion. Just wanted to go to church, any church without any church drama from anyone.

This Sunday, I would be in a place I did not know much about or much about anybody and what they did or didn't do. What should I wear? I didn't want to be overdressed. I didn't want to look like I was needy. Digging in the closet, I found a nice dark brown dress with a black design in it. My black flats, black purse, and my own rosary the couple gave me.

10:25 AM

All ready to go, Mass didn't start till 11 am I wanted to get there early to pray the rosary. I sat in the back due to my unfamiliarity of certain things in the Catholic church. I thought there were about thirty people here today and not a sound as the rosary was prayed. During Mass, it was very in order. No backtalking, no nonsense, everyone was in the reading and their normal Catholic tradition.

1 PM

On my way out, I was stopped by the couple that invited me. After all this time, I did not think they would even remember me. They were so glad to see me. They were the sweetest couple I had met in a long time. We talked for a while, I was asked to come over and have tea with them sometime. We said our goodbyes, and I was on my way home.

When I got in the house, I took my dress off and put on a pair of blue jeans and t-shirt. I didn't plan on going anywhere else, so why not> I did my house cleaning, washing of a few clothes, and organized my bedroom. My other bedroom, I used it for my crafts as well. And it was always junky no matter how I tried to keep it organized. My grandmother was never fond of doing any work on Sunday, but this was the only day I loved to clean.

I got so caught up in my work, I had to stop and make me a peanut butter sandwich with a glass of milk. After my sandwich, I turned on some soft jazz music and went to my recliner for a nap. The music was so relaxing, it took me to another time. Times like this I enjoyed. Times like this I valued. Times like this I didn't want to end.

8 PM

WOW, that was more than a nap. I got up, turned off all the lights, didn't have enough energy to finish my work. I could not keep my eyes open at all. Maybe all the organizing of my crafts did it. Folding material and putting labels on everything was a challenge. Before I knew it, I was asleep.

2 AM

Awakened by the same noise followed by footsteps. The footsteps were getting closer and closer. I could not move. My arms, legs, and head had no feeling, the more I tried to move my body, the covers would paste me to the bed. The only thing I could do was blink and move my eyes.

As the footsteps got closer, I began to have a panic attract. I could not breathe. I closed my eyes and quietly called the name Jesus repeatedly. The footsteps began to move away until they stopped. My covers released me.

I jumped up, grabbed my inhaler, took two breaths, looked down the hallway. Walked to the second bedroom, opened the closet, the living room, the kitchen, the storage room, the patio. All doors were locked and secured. I couldn't go back to bed, I sat in the living room on the sofa the rest of the morning. My mine wondering, what is happening and why, am I losing my sanity?

6 AM

I could not focus on my morning at all. I couldn't shower or eat. I finally got dressed, I had to get out of the house. With my mind spinning, a walk would do. I didn't think it would be a good thing to drive.

I walked on the walking trail near our homes to help clear my thoughts. I prayed I was not going through another breakdown. The first one was bad due to the physically and mental abuse from Ray. During the abuse, I started hearing noises and misplacing things. Maybe I needed to go back to my psychiatrist.

Anyway, it was Monday, I had no reason to go into the city. I had yardwork to do. Approaching my home, I took a deep breath, counted to ten, and started sweeping the fallen leaves. I worked two hours in the flowerbeds. Made me a glass of iced tea, went out to the patio and watched the workers work on the lake project.

12 PM

My lunch would be a simple hotdog and chips. I opened my storage room to get my chips. I looked around, thinking about the noise. I moved a few things, didn't know why or what I was going to see or find in such a small room, but hoping to find something. After my lunch I went to my desk to finish with my Bible reading.

I took notes on a few things, I needed to ask questions when I got to Bible class. I had all my Bible resource books to use and study but going to Bible study helped break it down to my understanding. Plus, I enjoyed the homework Father Jacobs gave for us to do by the next class. I told Father Jacobs about my 2 am wakeups. He told me to pray my rosary before I went to bed, Lord knows I needed to get the rest.

6 PM

Another hotdog and chips for dinner. Still amazed at the work being done on the lake project. I took my dinner out to watch. It was getting late; Gladys was bringing over a basket full of sandwiches and water to the workers. The workers stopped working, stood around laughing and talking as they ate.

8 PM

As the cool night air came in with the stars gave a beautiful sight, and to look up and see God's work gave me peace. I went to my room, got dressed for the night, and went to my recliner. The night was pleasant, and I was very relaxed in my thoughts. I watched the night sky as I drifted off to sleep.

Kim

2 AM

Footsteps again, "REALLY!" I said out loud. I got my rosary and as I prayed, I went to the storage room. Once again nothing, I went back to my recliner with no fear, prayed the rosary again. I didn't check the doors. I didn't have a panic attack. After the rosary prayer I had a peaceful sleep.

6 AM

At church I signed up for Tuesday mornings, to go to the nursing home and help the arts and craft activity instructor for the ones attending. Said my prayers for my morning, got dressed. Turned on the coffee pot, poured cereal and milk in a bowl. As I stood standing, eating my cereal, watching the coffee pot, thinking about the crafts and counting my supplies in my head. After my breakfast, I put my bowl in the sink, gathered up my supplies, and started out.

On my way into the city I called my cousin Kim. I really needed to talk to someone. We didn't talk much; she always told me the reason why bad things happened to me was because of my choices in life. And that I was too naïve, and that I didn't know how to pick good friends and good men for a relationship. Even though she put me down a lot, I had to call her. She answered the phone.

"Hello?"

"Hi, Kim, it's me, Rebecca, how are you?"

"Hi, Rebecca, do you know Ray has been blowing up my phone looking for you?"

"Kim, I am so sorry about that."

"Rebecca, he stopped calling after I told him I didn't know where you had run off to."

"Kim, will it be okay if I stopped by?"

"Sure, Rebecca, see you in a few."

Kim had never had a bad friendship or bad relationship. Kim believed that you chose what happened in your life. I didn't choose for my father to abuse me at a young age. I didn't choose for Ray to do the things he did. After thinking about all that, maybe I should call her back and tell her I would visit another time. "NO," maybe things would be different.

I pulled up at her home, got out, rang the doorbell, Kim came to the door, beautiful as ever. Kim had been married for twenty-five years with two kids, adults now. Married a wonderful husband who treated her like a queen, that I believe every woman should have. Kim welcomed me in and wanted to know what was on my mind. I told her all about my 2 am experiences, all at once, she laughed out loud and said, "Girl, you need help."

Kim had stopped my conversation and started talking about how she had moved up on the job. The plans for remodeling their home, and how well the kids were doing. She talked for an hour, until she focused back on me and said, "Sweetie, you never did tell me what was troubling you." I told her nothing, I just wanted to come visit and check on her and the family. Another hour passed with Kim saying if I had her smarts I would not have ended up in a bad marriage.

Hurting inside, I kept my smile on my face as I sat and listening to my cousin. Eventually I had enough, told her I had to go, we said our goodbyes. I had learned whom not to express my feelings to. Headed to the nursing home, I refused to let my depression show around these people. I was there to show and give love.

Most of their families didn't come to visit and I was all some of them had. Counting to ten, I focused only on my day. Walking around the nursing home, visiting and seeing who was able to come to class, brought joy to my heart. The nurse's aide helped me get my supplies out of the car, I was so thankful he was on break. Most of all, he helped with setting up the recreation room for the residents that would be attending.

My tables were set, men would be making coffee mugs, and the women cards for the occasion of their choice. As each one arrived, they each gave me a hug, I even got a few kisses on the cheek. If they only knew how much I needed all their love. They began to work on their crafts, I listened to their stories they told as they worked. It was like enjoying my grandparents all over again.

3 PM

I would be eating dinner at the nursing home today. Of course, the food was not good, but healthy for me. The satisfaction of laughing and talking would help. Dinner was over, everyone returned to their rooms. I cleaned the recreation area, did my paperwork for everyone that attended the craft activity. I took my time loading up my car. It was hard to leave; I got so attached to them quickly.

5 PM

On my way home I glanced over at the craft store. Surprised to see it was still open. This was one store I could stay in for hours. The store had 50%-off sales ads on the door. I had to go back to the car and get my Visa for this, I was not going to be able to control myself.

I could use more crafts for the seniors at the nursing home. Lace, buttons, wood, plastic, paints, yarn, thread, needles, and cardboard. I strolled down each section of the craft store. Found things for me, which would be added to my collection of crafts that I had not started on. By the time I got to check out, my buggy was full. The store gave me so much joy, like a kid in a candy shop.

7 PM

Two hundred and thirteen dollars with a savings of one hundred and fifty. I think I did good. I organized the trunk of the car before I placed my shopping bags in. The last bag I put in the back seat, my personal crafts. As I turned around to take my buggy back, a man's voice called out, "I will take it."

And of all people, it was Sam from the market. Sam trying to make conversation by saying he didn't see me much at the market or in the city. With my trust issues, I told Sam I didn't get out unless needed. He reached in his wallet, pulled out a card, and said, "Call at your convenience," then he walked away. Now, with my experience that was a man that wanted some play and I was not the one.

9 PM

What a day, too tired to unload the car. Inside the house I went, kicked off my shoes, flopped down in my recliner. Off into a deep sleep I went. After my nap, I unloaded the car. All my goodies went to the living room. Before putting them away, I had to admire my findings. I got a tote to put crafts in for the nursing home and the rest in a bag for my personal crafts.

11 PM

Tonight, I had a long shower. The warm water hitting my back and shoulders was like being at the massage therapist. No pajamas tonight, needed my body to breathe. I went to my dresser, took a nightgown out, got my cell phone, and went to my room. I took my bag of crafts and organized them with my other crafts.

Made a list of what all I had and what all I could make. I pulled a journal out of my desk and began to write about my day. My journal should be used every day. If I could write a book, I would have many stories to tell. Yeah, me, a writer, that's funny.

I can see it now; I would be laughed at by publishers. After playing around with my crafts and journal, I went to the kitchen, put a roast with potatoes, carrots, onion, and celery in my crockpot to cook overnight. I have a freezer, so I planned to cook meals and freeze so all I had was to pull and heat. My recipe book needed some attention, so I placed it on my craft table to redo in the future. Times like this I thought about my grandmother.

My grandmother taught me many things. As she sat and talked, I would watch and learn her techniques and the way she worked. Knitting and crocheting were the hardest to learn to do. While going to school, my mind was more on Grandmother than school. Grandmother would work from 4 am to 9 pm every day as a housekeeper for a family.

One day my mom was getting me ready for school, I didn't want to go. I overheard the day before that Grandmother would be off the next day. I wanted to spend my day with Grandmother. So, I pretended to be sick, my stomach hurting, my head hurting, I cried, and I used a marker and put little red dots on my arm for that extra help to keep me home. I played my mom so well, she called work, told them she would be late. When Grandmother came in my mom went to work.

Grandmother went to the bathroom, ran some water in the tub. Grandmother called for me to come in, take my clothes off, and gave me a nice bath, singing to me and telling me everything was going to be all right. Grandmother left the bathroom, came back with a belt in hand and I got it.

The Call

After my punishment, I had a long nap. When I woke up, I was able to learn how to sew. That was the good old days. Well, enough remembering good times, I prayed my rosary and went to bed.

2 AM

The sound of my cell phone awakened me, I answered the call. A whisper on the other end, I couldn't understand. I said hello again, all I heard was a faint laugh and the caller hung up the phone. The phone rang again. "Hello?" I said, no one spoke, another faint laugh, I hung up the phone and grabbed my rosary.

I sat up in bed. The laugh sounded like Ray. But how could that be? He did not have my new number. I got the phone, looked at the number, it said private number. What if Ray had found me? I got up, checked my doors and windows. I could not go back to sleep, I got my journal and wrote what I just experienced. I sat in my recliner the rest of the morning, hoping it was the wrong number and not Ray.

This was crazy, every morning at 2 am What was going on? Why every morning at 2 am I was awakened by something? Was I really losing it? I must be. There was no way, every morning at 2 A.M., this couldn't be going on for real. My medications should be in my system by now. It would seem more logical if things were happening at different times of the day and night, not just 2 am every time. This was not right. This was not true events, it just couldn't be.

6 AM

Still confused, I took my medication, fixed a light breakfast, and sat back in my recliner. Today was not going to be a good day. I must bring myself out of this. I had to get through this. I had to stay focused. After breakfast I went outside to watch the workers working on the lake. It was much cooler out today. Fall was leaving, winter was coming in. It would be the summer before we could enjoy the full pleasure of the lake.

William and Peggy were at the lake with a truck form their flower store. Looked like they were telling the workers to plant some bushes nearby. On their way from the lake they pulled up to my home, asked if I would like to have a rose bush planted in my yard. I walked over to the truck and picked out a rose bush to put in front of the bay window. William whistled for one of the workers to come over and plant the bush. As the workers planted, Peggy and I talked about how pretty the lake would be when it was finished.

I had such wonderful neighbors, life was so good here. Why couldn't I get myself together mentally? I was afraid to talk to them about what was going on. There was no telling how they would respond or if they would treat me differently. How would I even start to tell them? No, I needed to keep this to myself.

Sims

With the help of Jesus, I was going to see myself through this, bible study night is tonight, I needed to study. I highlighted and jotted down a few notes from the previous study.

8 AM

I went to the kitchen, turned on the coffee pot. Took my shower, found a comfortable pair of blue jeans, a nice gray top I bought early in the week, and my gray tennis shoes for my interview at the Sims. I needed to have the right clothing on just in case I was working today. This way I could bend in all the right places if I must do any lifting. As I sipped on my coffee, I still wondered about the calls early this morning.

I needed to get my mind off the phone calls and focus on my day. I couldn't go to an interview with my thoughts far away because it would show. I went outside, closed my eyes, took two deep breaths, and counted slowly to ten. Added water to the birdbath and birdseed to the feeder, went to the glider to watch the birds come in for the morning feeding. Put a letter in the mailbox, thanking the nursing home for having me come do crafts.

9 AM

Got my purse, notebook, and keys for my twenty-minute drive to the city. I was not sure of the address, I typed it in my navigating system, didn't want to take any chances on being late. The busy traffic would be long gone out of my way, which would give me a little relaxation on the way. When I made my turn off the dirt road onto the city road, my neighbor Bill headed my way with another truck full of supplies.

9:29 AM

I arrived at the Sims' home. I pulled up in the driveway, a man came to open my car door. With his pleasant voice, he said, "Good morning, Ms. Rebecca, I'm Jeff, I am so glad you came." Walking with Jeff, I looked around the outside of the home. Two-story home, well taken care of.

The shrubbery in front of the house was shaped in tulips. The landscaping to the front door was white stone lined with white marble rocks. A white stone wall that ran along the house, a flowerbed with many types of beautiful flowers. Jeff opened the door to an English Victorian home. Looked like something out of a magazine.

Mrs. Sims, Jeff's mother, age 94, sitting in the breakfast room having coffee with her legs crossed, watching TV. Jeff explained all she really needed was the companionship, assistance to doctor's appointments, cooking, washing of clothes, changing of the bed, assistance with baths, and light housecleaning. The upstairs she did not use due to fall risk. Jeff went up once a month to flush the toilets. Jeff had a family of his own and was not able to be at both places.

Jeff took me to the back of the house, where I was greeted by a German Shepherd named Lucky. Mrs. Sims lived alone so Jeff got Lucky for her to feel safe at night.

Mrs. Sims, a thin, slim lady, would be no problem with assisting in baths. The hours would vary due to Mrs. Sims' wants and needs. Jeff took me to the breakfast room and introduced me to Mrs. Sims. She asked did I know how to crochet, knit, and cross-stitch. I told her yes, those were my favorite crafts when I was sitting around the house.

Mrs. Sims told me when I came back to bring my crafts and supplies. That was a good sign for me, she wanted me back. After my interview, Jeff asked if I could start Monday at 9:30 am I told him yes. Jeff said he could only pay thirteen an hour cash, I told him that was fine. Jeff waved me goodbye as I pulled off.

12 PM

For once in a long time, the traffic and city life did not bother me. Just out of the blue, I turned my car into Momma Jo's Soul Food Restaurant. I felt I could mingle with others, eating alone would be weird, I could do this. On Fridays most places were busy, that didn't stop me. I got out, went in, the waiter gave me a table at the window, which was perfect.

I ordered sweet tea while I looked over the menu. The restaurant was family owned, very clean, and workers smiling as they worked. I made up my mind to order the steak, baked potato, steamed carrots, and salad. While I ate, I glanced around the restaurant, noticed I wasn't the only one eating alone, and it didn't bother me that I was. After my meal, I was ready to get home and write in my journal.

1 PM

On my way home I passed by four dump trucks filled with dirt. They must be coming from our field. I turned on the dirt road, four more dump trucks leaving with dirt, yes, that was from the field. As I got near my home, I looked over to the once field. The hole was so wide and deep, looked like a huge meteoroid had fallen and left its mark. All five families would be having a meeting tomorrow at Bill's home on further plans concerning the lake. Every house would bring a dish, my dish was a beef roast. Bill and Gladys, a fruit tray, Paul and Linda, fresh-baked cookies, Floyd and Wendy, vegetable casserole, William and Peggy, rolls and tea. I was looking forward to meeting. We had so much fun when we were all together.

I took my time going home just to see the lake. I opened the door, placed my keys on the desk, fixed a glass of tea so I could study before Bible class tonight. I found my black tote bag to put my Bible, notebook, folder, pen, and markers in. The tote made it easier with the three sections inside. On the front of the tote had a section for my cell phone and reading glasses.

Back out the door, I headed to St. Paul's. When I arrived my other five classmates were sitting in the car, waiting on the door to the classroom to open. I enjoyed Bible class, no matter if it was Baptist or Catholic. I would like to take a course online at the college in writing and English. Lord knows I needed help in that area. Now when I was younger, Mother could not get me to read, study, or anything. I barely made it out of my senior year. Not until I started going to the junior college did I change. Life looked different, I was different, all at once I wanted to turn back the hands of time and redo high school.

5 PM

Father Jacobs opened the door to the classroom. Tonight's lesson was on Christian faith. Handouts were place at each chair on the big round table. A projector was set up for a showing of the lesson plan and a short story form the Bible. Father Jacobs always had snacks to give during Bible class.

After Bible class we didn't hang around, it was cold outside. Everyone ready to get home and get warm. When I left Ray it was snowing, came here to fall weather, now it was snowing. It was like having two winters in one year. I did have a couple of plants I needed to put in the shed.

I got home, too tired to take a shower, I put on my gown, laid on my bed. I woke up to go to the bathroom and check my doors. I set my alarm clock to go off at 1:30 am I refused to be awakened at 2 am Jumped back into bed and off to sleep I went.

Dark Shadow

2 AM

I was awakened by a feeling of someone watching me. My back towards the door of my bedroom, my face to my dresser mirror. I looked in the mirror, saw a dark shadow beside my bed behind me. The shadow didn't move. Terrified, I made a little sound with my mouth to see if it would move, no movement.

I then decided to stretch, when I did the shadow figure eased out of my bedroom. I eased up out of bed to hear movement and footsteps. Not a sound could be heard. I waited ten minutes or more before I got up. I got my flashlight and hammer, went towards the front.

I turned on every light in the house, checking my doors, closets, and windows, nothing at all. I checked my bedside clock to see why the alarm didn't go off at 1:30 am It was unplugged. How could it be unplugged, when I set it just before I went to bed? I opened the back door to see if I could see any footprints, none to see. I opened the front door to see if I could see any footprints, none to see.

I sat at the kitchen table, unsure of myself and the events that had just happened. A sound of something fell, came from the shed outside. I didn't move. I prayed out loud. I got my rosary. All I could do was call on the name of Jesus. I sat in my same spot till daylight.

7 AM

In a hurry to put my clothes on, I rushed out to the shed to see what had fallen. The door was unlocked. I had forgotten to lock the door from the last time I was in the shed. I opened the door, my yard broom was on the floor with a broken flowerpot. I looked down to find footprints on the ground that led to the woods behind my home. I saw my neighbor Bill outside, I called for him to come over. I explained my 2 am wakeup after I showed him the footprints and the shed. Bill got on his cell phone, called his wife Gladys, and told her the story. Bill said, "We will discuss this problem today at the meeting."

9 AM

I was so glad I told Bill about my morning, without the footprints for proof I wouldn't have told him for fear he wouldn't believe me. After Bill left, I went back into my home and started working on my beef roast for our meeting today. I felt so much safer since I let Bill know what had happened. Drinking my coffee, I sat thinking of what to wear to the neighborhood meeting. It was cold outside, I pulled out my black boots, blue jeans, and a black pullover sweater.

Once I got dressed, I went to the back of the house, followed the footprints into the woods. I didn't go too far, just enough till I was uncomfortable. The more I followed, the prints faded along with the morning dew. I turned around and began to walk back to my home. The woods were pretty during the day, at night the woods looked scary. Maybe I should put a fence up to separate me from the woods.

The Meeting

11 AM

My beef roast was ready to be placed in my food container. I cleaned the stove, washed up my cooking pan, and made me one more cup of coffee before I went to the meeting at Bill and Gladys' home. The meeting was held at their home because it was the biggest home in the neighborhood. Gladys' living room was large like a conference room. Which made it easy to have sitting and food all in one area.

I grabbed my food container off the counter and left for Bill and Gladys' home. I took my time walking to their home. I wanted to be the last one there, I wanted to give Bill time to talk to my neighbors before I arrived. I didn't want to talk about my morning again. As I walked in the house, everyone was there.

I placed my food with the other food and got me another cup of hot coffee. Bill and Gladys walked over and explained that they had called the neighbors to come over a little early to talk about what happened at my place. I was so thankful Bill took that off me to do. Bill stated he would be getting me an alarm system in today. Bill told me not to worry, he would be showing me how to use the system.

Paul and Linda walked over and said they were worried because I lived alone, and would it be okay if they asked their son to put a fence around my backyard. I told them I thought about a fence this morning, and that I would love to have one. Paul got his cell phone, called his son, who owned the local fencing company, to make an appointment to come out and see the place for fencing. Linda assured me that I would enjoy the fence and I would feel safer. I gave my blessing and thanks to them both.

Floyd and Wendy came my way, said they were terrified about what happened this morning. The couple asked if they could get me a camera installed at the back and front door. I did not turn them down, I was thankful. Floyd said I could check my computer every morning to see if anyone had been out on the front or back porch. Plus, the cameras rotated a little to give more footage.

Last, William and Peggy walked over to me with a hug from each. William gave me a small box, I opened it. In the box was a small gun. William said he would be teaching me how to shoot the gun. Peggy smiled and said I would feel safe with protection in hand. I gave them my thanks.

Before we said our grace and ate, I had to get up and share my thanks to my neighbors. I let them know how thankful I was to have such good friends as neighbors. I thanked them for opening their homes to me and treating me as if I were their own. As I continued to talk my eyes got watery. After my little thank-you, I walked around the table and gave hugs.

As we fixed our plates and ate, we talked about plans for the lake. Bill said we would have a large cemented area for recreation by the lake. Gladys mentioned the nice metal outdoor chairs and tables. Paul ordered a large grill and smoker. Linda wanted a cooking table for prep near the grills. Floyd and Wendy ordered two tin trashcans. William and Peggy ordered pedal boats. Last, I ordered the outdoor lighting for night. After agreement on each idea, we now had an outdoor kitchen.

We fellowshipped a while after talking about the lake. I stayed and helped Gladys clean and get her living room and kitchen back in order. It did me a lot of good to be around others with a kind heart. Took my mind off negative things. Bill gathered up all the trash and headed to the back door, with a beer in the other hand. Gladys and I took a cup of coffee and sat at the kitchen table, exchanging recipes.

3 PM

I said my goodbyes to Bill and Gladys. Bill and Gladys said they and the alarm company would be over at 5 pm My walk home was pleasant,

I was at peace knowing my neighbors knew about this morning and all the help and love they gave and showed put a smile on my face. I got home, put the small gun under my bed till William could show me how to use it. I looked around to make sure my place was in order before guests arrived.

Before I could finish touching up my home, Bill and the alarm company were at the door. When I opened the door Bill wasted no time, he took the man around to the back door, showed him all the windows, I did not have to say a word. Soon Gladys came over, we sat in the living room talking while Bill watched and talked with the man from the alarm company. I was feeling safer already, knowing Bill and Gladys were overseeing the alarm system job. I should be able to sleep on past 2 am

Gladys asked if she could walk to my shed and see if any footprints were left. I pointed to the shed door and the ground, the broken pot still on the floor. Gladys walked in the shed and looked around, with a worried look I asked was she okay. Gladys wanted to know if I noticed the sleeping bag and blanket under the worktable in the back of the shed. I walked over, got on my hands and knees, looked like someone used to sleep there.

Gladys called for Bill to come out and see our findings. Bill informed us that the previous owners had a son that liked to come out to the shed to smoke and drink. He would sometimes stay all night out in the shed. Bill's story eased my mind. We walked back to my home and Bill demonstrated how to use the alarm system.

I walked Bill and Gladys to the door, set my alarm early. I went to my bedroom, got ready for a long, hot bath. During my bath all my worries washed away. I played back the day, thoughts about the lake, how concerned my neighbors were, and how helpful they were. Soon I dozed off, in relaxation. I dreamed I was outside naked, and the wind was cool, finally I woke up to a cold tub of water.

Jumping out of the tub, I rushed to dry off and put my night clothes on. It was still early, I did not care, I was full of food from our meeting and ready for real sleep. I checked my doors and the alarm system one more time before bed. Got my rosary said my prayer, into my bed I went. I enjoyed watching the evening sky as I relaxed, soon I was asleep.

The Footprints

2 AM

Awakened by a noise at my bedroom window. It sounded like someone trying to open it. I sat up in bed to see if I could see anything. I heard the sound again, I went to the window; I saw someone run. I jumped back so fast, I fell and hit my head on the nightstand. The fall left me unconscious. I finally woke up hours later.

6 AM

I got up off the floor, confused and remembering what happened. I went to the window to check; it was safe and secured. I eased my way to the kitchen to fix a cup of coffee. I sat at the table with no thoughts, no feelings, no nothing. Just there in confusion. After collecting myself, I got dressed and went outside to investigate.

I walked slowly to my bedroom window. There on the ground, footprints. Who could it be? What did they want or need? The shed door was slightly open, I went over, opened the door. I looked to see if anyone had been on the sleeping bag. I couldn't tell. The footprints from the window led into the woods, I wanted to follow but I was too scared.

Should I call Bill and Gladys? No, no, this would sound weird. Maybe the prints were there from the night before and I missed them. Just maybe I fell out of bed and dreamed I heard the noise at the window. I sat on the back porch, holding my arms, looking into woods. Could there be someone out there watching me?

I went inside, called the number to my psychiatrist. I needed to see Mrs. Waters today if I could. I was in luck, a cancelation, which made an opening for me at 11 am this morning. I didn't care how I dressed today, I just needed Mrs. Waters. I fixed a cup of coffee and pen to write down the events that happened.

11 AM

After my coffee, I wasted no time to get to Mrs. Waters. I sat anxiously, waiting on my name to be called. Finally, I was called back, I didn't give Mrs. Waters time to speak, I started telling what happened. This time Mrs. Waters didn't take notes, she looked me in the eyes as I told my story. She didn't stop me from talking, only listened.

Finally, I was finished with my story. Mrs. Waters sat back in her chair and looked at me for at least two minutes. Mrs. Waters stated that with my mental illness I could be experiencing hallucinations. Which was a perception of having seen, heard, or touched something that wasn't there. And the reason for my fall, I got up out of bed quickly, the medication caused dizziness. I had to ask for her to explain the footprints, by the window and the shed door.

Mrs. Waters said, "Remember the workers that are working on the lake, they could have made the footprints or the man that installed the alarm system." Mrs. Waters did make a lot of sense of my story. I was glad I didn't go to Bill and Gladys. Mrs. Waters gave me a stronger medication to help me sleep at night, Lord knows I needed it. Mrs. Waters told me to start keeping a journal on my events and to drink less coffee. I did feel better after my talk with Mrs. Waters.

On my way home, I stopped by the library and checked out books I could find on bipolar schizophrenia disorder. I couldn't wait to get home to study in the books I checked out. As I pulled in my yard, I saw two of the workers carrying wood to the back of my yard. I asked what they were doing. I was told they were instructed to carry cut wood to the end of the lots near the woods for Bill.

"Thank you," I said to the workers. I was so relieved, I now found the source of my footprints. I took my books inside, fixed another cup of coffee, and went out on the front to watch the workers. It was always relaxing to see the construction of the lake. In a month or two the fire department would come and fill the lake with water from the two fire hydrants we had near the homes. Which would cause our bills to be a little higher for each month, we all did agree on using the fire department and city water to fill the lake.

The Symptoms

Enough of watching workers build the lake, I needed to study my books. I cleaned my desk, made room for my library books, and pulled out a new notebook to take notes in. I had read on my mental illness before, but it seemed like I had forgotten my symptoms. My first book, *Bipolar Disorders*, first chapter, explained manic depression, an emotional breakdown. I had three in my life so far.

I remembered my first emotional breakdown was in my childhood years, with my father's abuse towards me and my mother. The second breakdown was the chemical spill at work. And my third, marriage with Ray. It was hard to turn off the negative. Being hard on myself, learned by words of negative forced at me. All the negative made me think that was what and whom I really was.

The chapter also stated that I might have mood swings. Yes, I did. One moment I could be all happy, next moment I would be sad. Not only that, I could be very high with excitement and happiness followed by depression and guilt. Just like my plan and excitement of always wanting to be a famous author, I could feel unstoppable in my goal but easily distracted. The manic parts were my racing thoughts.

Sometimes it is difficult to focus on one thing, and I always overanalyzed my thoughts, just like the book said. I had so many stories I had started on, one completed, one halfway down, others I had started but couldn't seem to move forward with publishing due to negative thoughts. So, what if I didn't become a famous author, so what if no one liked my writings? Just write and do it already. But easier said and done.

Chapter Two, "Irritation," switching from one extreme to the other before returning to my euphoric stage. Just like now I was getting agitated by reading all this, time for a break from my studies. I closed my book and notebook, all the reading gave me a slight headache. As I walked to the kitchen, my doorbell rang. It was Greg, Paul and Linda's son. He said he would be working on putting my new fence up in the morning.

I walked around the house with Greg, watching as he took notes. He asked did I want a chain-link fence or a private fence. I was not sure, so he gave me a booklet with pictures of different styles of fencing. I told Greg to meet me at his parents' home when he was finished at my place. As I walked, I glanced over the booklet, I didn't want to make the house look bad by putting up the wrong fence, that was why I needed Paul and Linda.

A nice sweet smell hit me in the face as I approached Paul and Linda's home. The smell of peanut butter cookies made my mouth water. I rang the doorbell; Linda came to the door with smiles. I couldn't wait to get inside to be near those cookies. First thing out of Linda's mouth, "Would you like a cookie and a glass of milk?"

And I did not turn her down. Paul and Linda sat with me at the table, we ate cookies and looked at fences. I let Paul make the decision on the fence, Linda and I were involved in cookie recipes. Soon Greg came in, took a seat, we all laughed and talked, eating cookies and deciding which fence would look good. Finally, a chain-link fence was chosen for my home.

As we continued to talk, we heard a loud crash in the field where the lake was being constructed. We all ran outside to see what was going on. The loud crash caused all the neighbors to go outside to investigate. All the workers were gathered around each other, we could hear them talking loud but could not understand them. Paul, Bill, Floyd, William, and Greg ran over to the worksite.

Linda, Gladys, Wendy, Peggy, and I waited and watched patiently to see. The guys returned, told us that one of the trucks had overturned into the lake and no one was hurt. A crane would be here tomorrow to pull the truck out. It was good to know no one was hurt or injured. The man that was driving the truck came back with the guys. They wanted to make sure he was okay before he left to go home.

I went back in to see if I could help do anything, as I got closer, I noticed the man, it was Sam from the market. I walked over to ask if he was okay, he said he was and thanked me for my concerns. I went to the kitchen to help Linda, we prepared soup and a sandwich for Sam to eat as he talked with Paul. Linda told me Sam did a lot of volunteer work around the city, served in the military also. I learned that Sam had been married before, had no children, and enjoyed helping others.

All that I learned about Sam made me feel bad because of the way I had judged him. Thank God he didn't know my thoughts of him, the day I ran my buggy into him at the market or the day he gave me his number. Linda and I cleaned up the kitchen and went into the living room with Paul and Sam to see if they needed anything. I said goodbye to them all and headed back to my home. Greg walked with me and said he would be back sometime next week to start the fence. I thanked him as he left.

6 PM

I got home, I set my bedside alarm clock for 1:30 A.M., took a long bath, made some hot tea, got my bock on schizophrenia, and got into bed to read. First chapter talked about unusual thoughts or suspicions; this I did: "Expresses false illogical thinking, increased clumsiness, difficulty thinking clearly, don't maintain constant eye contact and social withdrawal." All these things I did, sometimes I realized it, sometimes I didn't. I closed the book, turned off the lamp, and looked at the wall until I was asleep.

A Shadow or Ray

Alarm went off at 1:30 am I got up with a smile on my face, I was not going to let 2 am wake me up this time. I went to the kitchen for a peanut butter cracker. I sat at the table, looking at my to-do list and my list of things to keep me busy during the day. I made a new list, organizing with things I knew I wouldn't change my mind on doing.

Last I made a list of things I needed to get at the market. I went to my food closet to see if I needed any canned goods, went over to the washer to check my laundry detergent and bleach. I noticed my washer had been pulled out a little and the little door to the small room was open. That was weird, maybe Bill did it when he was showing the alarm system installer around. I pushed the washer back against the small door, cleaned the kitchen table of my notes.

2 AM

I turned off the kitchen light and headed back to the bedroom. As I walked, I felt someone behind me someone looking at me. I turned around, there was a shadow at the front door. A shadow of a person. I was frightened, I could not move. The shadow started to come closer and closer. I didn't know what to do so I reached for my vase and threw it at the shadow.

The vase hit the floor, the shadow backed away, out the open front door it went. I ran to the door, stepping on broken glass to close it. I closed the door, wondering why and how the door got unlocked and open. Why did I forget to set the alarm system? But I set the alarm early and checked the doors early. Could this be one of my symptoms I had read about?

I stood with my back to the door, my feet bleeding from the broken vase, I just stood still. I was not sleeping this time; I was not sleeping this time. Could I be making something false into reality? I remember reading that in one of the books. But why was the door opened? I closed and locked it when I came home. Or did I?

Thirty minutes had passed before I moved. I had to get myself together, this was all in my head. My books said things like this could happen with my illness. I made it to the bathroom to remove glass from my feet and apply alcohol, ointment, and wrap both feet. I got my rosary to pray and meditate on God's word, forcing all negativity away from my mind.

Before I went back to my bedroom, I cleaned and picked up the broken vase. I made it back to bed but did not sleep. I knew I was safe here. I just had to get my mental illness under control and I could do this. Like Mrs. Waters said, once my new medication got into my system I would feel and see the difference. My home was quiet, I was finally at ease again in a way.

I couldn't stop thinking about Ray. What if it was Ray doing these things to me? What if he paid off my lawyer to find me? NO, that was another symptom, making more out of something than it was. Okay, I needed some rest from the monsters inside of my head, plus I was talking to myself now.

Jesus, I believed I was answering myself, too. I covered my head and prayed myself to sleep. I didn't sleep long, it was still dark at 4 am I laid in bed looking up at the ceiling, wondering if I should sign up for group. Maybe talking about this with others that were going through the same thing would help. Then just maybe I could learn how to separate reality from hallucinations. Hopefully I could meet someone who had learned how to control this thing.

8 AM

I got up out of bed, got dressed, went to the service station, purchased a prepaid cell phone. The phone would allow me to make a call by using a different area code for location. I returned home, pacing the floor till I had enough nerve to call Ray's sister. The phone rang, I told her who I was and asked if she had seen or heard from Ray. She said the family had not heard or seen Ray, he told them he was going on a vacation.

She said Ray left for vacation two days after I went missing. I didn't give her time to finish, I hung up the phone. Had he found me? What would he do to me? Should I tell someone? NO, they would think I was crazy.

There was no way Ray knew where I was, no way. I went outside to check my home. Windows okay, doors okay, shed okay, and then I thought about the little room. I wondered if there was a door on the outside of my home leading into that little room. I walked around to the back, looking down, and noticed a small door, but only a small child could get through that. I opened it and it did lead to the small area behind the washer.

I went to the shed, got two pieces of wood that were going to be used for a bookshelf, and a drill with eight screws in my hand. I moved the washer, opened the small door, crawled inside the little area with my wood and drill. I made it to the door on the other side, placed the two wood pieces, and drilled them in place. Nothing could get in now. I went back outside to look at my work. I opened the small door and no way in.

The work I did made me tired, I fixed a cup of coffee and went to the front porch. I didn't notice how cool it was outside while I was working, my coffee warmed me up. I had plans to go to church today, but after talking to Ray's sister I wanted to stay home. I sat thinking about the fence, that would help me lot. Adding the fence would put security in my head.

I thought I might get the whole house fenced in, not just the back. That way I could lock the fence from the front near the mailbox. Maybe I would invest in a dog also after the fence went up. Having a dog around would keep me company also. By me living in the county and not the city, I would be able to get a pit or German Shepherd, have him trained for inside and outside.

Quickly my mind went back to Ray. What if it was Ray sleeping in the shed? What if it was Ray tormenting me at 2 am in the morning? All this just because I left him. Why would he do this when he had his secretary now? All the names he would call me. Telling me he would be better off without me. There was no way it could be Ray.

Another idea crossed my mind, I went to the shed, looked under the table to see if the sleeping bag was still there, and it was. I made a fold at the edge by the bottom of the sleeping bag near the wall. In the morning I would check it, if the fold was still there no one was sleeping in the bag, if the fold was gone then I had a problem. I then went to the small door, which led to the small area behind the washer, I placed a small string above the door, if it did not open the string would be in place, if the door got open the strings would fall. Now let's see what was really happening.

12 PM

Tomorrow I would be working for Mrs. Sims, I went to my craft area to fix my activity bag. I was so glad to hear Mrs. Sims tell me to bring my crochet, knit, and cross-stitching with me. I found many patterns Mrs. Sims might like. Before I left her home, I did a little looking around at things she had done in needlework, that helped in picking out what to pack in my bag. Finally, I chose a pattern for each project, added my needles, threads, other tools needed, and all ready to go.

I took my activity bag to the living room so I wouldn't forget it. Went to the kitchen to find something to eat. I was not all that hungry, so I decided to fix me a tuna salad sandwich and a glass of iced tea. Before I ate, I got my medication and took it, went out to my mailbox, got my newspaper, put it on the table by my recliner. After eating my sandwich, I took my tea to the living room and got all cozy in my recliner with the newspaper.

A lot of interesting things in the local paper today. A man hit by a truck outside a local store. Witness told police a man struck another man with his truck and took off. The victim was taken to the hospital and treated. Victim said he tried to jump out of the way but got struck anyway. Thank goodness the witness saw the truck's make, model, and tag.

The theatre in town was bringing a play to stage, *Annie*, following the original 1977 Broadway production. Show times Thursday and Friday 7:30 pm and Saturday at 5:30 pm Sounded like something I would like to do. The college was also having plays performed by local high schools during the week, Monday and Tuesday 5 pm Wednesday at 3 pm there would be a chili cookoff downtown, five dollars to taste each chili. Bingo Monday night through Friday 4 pm with many prizes to win.

I took a highlighter and highlighted all the events taking place next week, hoping I would be still interested in attending a few. The rest of the paper I just glanced over, sports not into, obituaries too sad, job listings not interested, police reports don't want to know, and homes, property, furniture for sale, don't need. The "mark your calendar" section was good with monthly events and different clubs meeting. To my surprise I found a volunteer section in the paper, help needed for the soup kitchen and shelter. Now that was something I must highlight; I enjoy helping others in need.

3 PM

Greg pulled up in the front yard with his truck full of supplies and behind him another truck with two men, whom I assumed to be Greg's workers. I met Greg outside to sign my paperwork on the fence. We agreed to have the fence surround the entire house, with a locked gate in front. I watched the workers work for a while before I went to Paul and Linda's home. I thought I should let Paul and Linda know my real reason for moving here. Just in case it was Ray and if something happened, they would at least have something to go by. What if they thought I was crazy? I must tell them anyway; I must for my safety.

As always, the smell of something sweet coming from their home as I got closer, this time it smelled like apples. I knocked on the door, Linda answered with a big smile. She welcomed me in, and I followed her to the kitchen with the smell of apples luring me in. Linda fixed tea and gave me a fresh-baked apple tart. Paul walked over to the table to join us as we talked.

I told Paul and Linda my story from beginning to end. I even told them I had called Ray's sister, to ask if she had seen him, and what his sister told me. Paul and Linda assured me that I was safe now and that my 2 am wakeups were just stress from my past and I needed to see a psychiatrist to help deal with it. I told them I was seeing Mrs. Waters. Paul said that she was the best in town. It did me good to let them know my past and about my 2 am wakeups. I didn't feel alone now.

6 PM

Greg knocked on the door to his parents' home and asked if I would come and see my new fence. Paul and Linda followed behind me to see his work. I rushed to my home with excitement, the closer I got I could see the fence and I was very pleased upon arrival. At the front of my home was an entrance to enter my gate. I opened the gate with the key Greg gave me, went inside, walked around my whole yard with gladness and admiring Greg's good work. I was so happy, I gave Greg a big hug and a thank-you. Greg smiled and said, "I never got a hug for putting up a fence." I said my goodbyes to Greg, Paul, and Linda and went inside. I opened the back door, stepped out, and looked around again at the fence. The fence made me feel even safer from the woods in the back of the property.

8 PM

After my excitement from the fence being installed, I decided to call William and Peggy about the gun they had given me. It didn't come with bullets and if it did, I didn't even know how to load the thing. And if it was loaded, I wouldn't know how to fire it. William said he would take me to the gun store tomorrow after work and then to the shooting range to get my license and practice aiming and shooting the gun.

9 PM

After my shower I put on a jogging set, my outfit, together for tomorrow. Tonight, I planned to stay up and watch my morning come in. I turned on every light in my home.

I didn't want to fall asleep with no lights on, I turned on every light so I could see every inch, corner, and closet in my home. I started my night off by reading, which was not a good idea at all. The book made me sleepy and I could not get focused or entertained in the first two chapters. Next, I tried doing some writing of my own. I pulled out my notes on my short stories and added more exciting pages. Once I got bored of that, I did whatever I could around the house to keep me up. Cleaning, rearranging furniture, looking at cookbooks and craft books.

10 PM

Fighting sleep was so hard. I didn't take my night medications so I wouldn't have to fight sleep, looked like my body had gotten used to my medication because it wanted to fight back and sleep. I went to the kitchen, made a turkey sandwich, and pulled out a cold Dr Pepper to give me energy. No movies or good TV shows on this time of night, only product advertising, and I didn't need to watch that, I would order things I didn't need.

11 PM

Thinking about how my workday would go with Mrs. Sims took my mind off the clock. I pulled out my bag, I paced by the door with my crafts, took everything out to make sure I had all my tools that were needed, and the things Mrs. Sims asked for me to bring. I added extra thread of different colors, if we did cross-stich or needlepoint I would have many colors to choose from. I placed my hot glue gun in my bag also, never knew when it could come in handy.

12 AM

Still fighting sleep, I walked over to my desk, pulled my journal out, and wrote about my day. Writing about the fence made me feel good. Paul and Linda had been such wonderful friends to me and very understanding, I had to add them to my journal for the day. After writing I pulled my to-do list out, scratched off and added on things I wanted to do and no longer wanted to do. Went back to the kitchen, got a freeze pop, walked around the house, seeing what ideas I could come up with to make the inside of my home look different. Maybe I could start a painting project for each room soon. I could feel my body getting tense, my anxiety rising as the time got closer to 2 am I needed to stay focused. But I kept thinking what was going to happen at 2 am I took the mop bucket and filled it with soap and water. I mopped the kitchen floor, refreshed my mop water, and mopped the bathroom floor. Turned on the ceiling fan to help dry the floor, rearranged my bookshelf and CD case.

2 AM

I sat still on the couch in the living room with my flashlight and hammer in my hand. At least I was up and ready for whatever was going to happen. With every light on no shadow could be seen. Or no person could stand still. Not a noise, not a sound from the trees as the wind lightly blew through the leaves. I did not move, I just listened, I just waited. My body started to shake. I waited to hear something. I waited to see something. Nothing, nothing, soon the hour had passed and it felt like the longest hour of my life.

3 AM

I made it, nothing happened, yes, yes, yes, maybe Paul was right, it was just stress from my past. I went back to my desk to write my morning down. This first good note I would have for Mrs. Waters. I thought my medication was finally working. Maybe I should sleep during the day and stay up during the night. I felt so good.

4 AM

Too excited to sleep now. I made some coffee, fixed me an egg, slice of bacon, and grits for my early morning breakfast. Opened my kitchen window, sat down to eat and watch the sunrise. After breakfast I took my morning medication, got a hot shower, put my clothes on for the day, did my hair and makeup. I opened the front door, walked to the mailbox to collect my newspaper, I noticed birds feeding in the birdfeeder, and a small bird with a nest and three eggs in the bush by the fence. Nature has always been my thing.

5 AM

I looked over to see if any workers had made it in to work on the lake, to my surprise I saw Sam so I gave him a wave. Sam waved back as he walked to me, eating something that looked like a biscuit. When Sam had arrived, his biscuit was gone. I offered Sam a cup of coffee, we sat on the porch to talk while he was waiting on Bill to arrive. As we talked, out of the blue Sam asked me out on a dinner date and cocktail afterwards. I said yes. And I was happy to say yes. I was ready to start trusting again.

7 AM

After Sam left I loaded up the car to go to work for the Sims. On my way to work I stopped by Paul and Linda's bakery for coffee but most of all to tell Linda about last night, that no strange things happened and that Sam asked me out. Linda jumped for joy at both my morning and night, we hugged and had coffee and talked about what I should wear tonight. I said my goodbyes and headed to work.

Workday

8 AM

When I arrived at the Sims' home, Lucky, the Sims' dog, met me in the driveway with his tail wagging and tongue hanging out. I loaded my things onto my small carrying rolling cart and went to the side door. I didn't have to ring the doorbell, Mrs. Sims was sitting at the kitchen table waiting on me. As I entered Mrs. Sims gave me a smile. Mrs. Sims was already eating her breakfast. Her son Jeff left me a note that all I had to do today was entertain his mom.

The home health aide had come out early and gave Mrs. Sims her bath, the light housework was done, and breakfast prepared. After reading my note I unloaded my cart and bag in the kitchen, arranged everything on the table so Mrs. Sims could see all the crafts I had and that she had asked me to bring.

Mrs. Sims asked if I could feed Lucky while she finished up her breakfast. Lucky was a very good dog, I had no problem with getting Lucky to obey me. I even gave him a treat for being a good dog. When I returned back to the kitchen, Mrs. Sims asked if I would go to the den and get her purple box sitting by her chair. The box was a clear purple, I could see all her needles, threads, and other craft supplies, looked like it was going to be a good day for us.

After Mrs. Sims finished her breakfast, I cleaned up the table so she could get her supplies out and find an activity for the day. After I finished the dishes and cleaned the kitchen, I returned to the table. Mrs. Sims chose to do needlepoint for today. As we worked on our needlepoint, she told me about her childhood life and how hard it was growing up with both parents sick.

Mrs. Sims said that Mama Jo's Restaurant would be making a lunch delivery to the house. Mrs. Sims pulled out a money bag from the kitchen drawer and gave me money for the order. Mrs. Sims said that the money was her play money. Jeff gave Mrs. Sims money every Friday for her to go shopping, eat out, or to just save.

1 PM

The doorbell rang, it was Mama Jo's Restaurant with lunch for two. Mrs. Sims and I had to move to the dining room table to eat. Our needlepoint work and supplies were all over the kitchen table. Mrs. Sims and I washed our hands and sat down to a nice double cheeseburger, slaw, and sweet potato fries. For a small lady, Mrs. Sims finished all her food with no problem. After lunch we returned to the kitchen to finish our needlepoint and talk.

Mrs. Sims and I had finished our needlework of flowers, next we would sew the needlework onto a pillowcase. Jeff came in at 3:30 P.M., time had gone by so fast. I didn't even realize it. Jeff walked me to the door and asked would I be back, I told him I would. Jeff gave me an envelope with money in it for my workday. I wasn't expecting to get my pay till the end of the work week but that was cool with me also.

I made a stop at the Bed and Go store to purchase four white pillowcases for Mrs. Sims' next project. While shopping I found a bed sheet with the same flowers Mrs. Sims and I had needlepointed, I had to buy it. The sheet would look good with the pillowcases, all we had to do was add a little lace around the sides and bottom to bring out the handcraft look to the sheet.

Gun Practice

4 PM

On my way home all I could think about was going to gun practice with William and Peggy. I have always been afraid of guns; guns make me so nervous, plus the thought of a gun can kill. I know it's good protection, but it can kill. I only needed something just to lay a predator out till help arrived. Like a taser or something. But I couldn't turn down my gift. I got home, changed into my blue jeans and t-shirt while I waited on my call from William and Peggy. I sat on the front porch watching Sam as he worked. Wondering what type of man he was. How would he treat me? Was he honest? All these things running inside my head as I watched him work.

Finally, I got a call from William and Peggy, said they were on their way. I got my gun case, locked up my home, and walked to the edge of my yard, locked the gate, and got into the car with William and Peggy. When we arrived at the gun range, I was able to get a gun permit and a card to use on the practice field. Before we went to the field, we went to the gun shop. So many guns of all sizes. Peggy and I walked over to another section of the shop, that was when I learned my gun was a 9mm. I saw girly guns, pink, purple, and blue with diamonds and pearls on the guns and the pouches to match. I asked if I could trade my all-black in for a pink gun, which didn't look so scary. After my trade the gun didn't look so scary.

Next, I had to go in a classroom for first-timers with a gun, watch a video, and take a test. The video was on gun safety and how to keep the gun safe. The second part of the video was about how dangerous a gun was, followed by a test on that section. The third part of the video was about basic gun care followed by a test. Now it was time for hands-on, which covered all I had learned on the videos.

I learned how to load, unload, and basic cleaning of the gun. Then we went to the field to practice shooting my gun. William said we had a week of training on gun basics. William did let me shoot few times and my aiming was so bad. Each time I fired the gun I moved back, and the gun went up. William assured me I would get better after more practices. On our way home we talked about the lake and couldn't wait till it was done. William said that Sam had a liking to me, so I told him we had a date tonight. Peggy was thrilled and said it would be wonderful for me and Sam to date. Peggy told me not to worry, Sam was a gentleman and had a big heart and I was in good hands.

The Date

6 PM

When I arrived home, I went to my bedroom, looked over the four outfits I had on my bed for tonight. All I had to do now was find shoes and a small purse to match. I put my hair up in a bun and light makeup, I didn't want to overdo anything. I thought I would wear my black and white polka-dot dress with black flats and my small black purse. After my shower I powdered my face, applied lotion to my body, and put on my bra and panties. As I sat on my bed, I felt good about the night to come. I had no fears. As I dressed for the night, I was very calm and full of self-esteem.

I remember when I first met Sam, I would not give him the time or day. I was scared to even look at a man, fear I would not be pleasing enough. I looked at Sam differently now, I don't know what changed in my head. I had no fear, I didn't care if I pleased him or not. Just wanted to enjoy my night and make the best out of it for me, not for him.

8 PM

I heard a car door as I put my shoes on. I went to the window, it was Sam and he looked nice, plus we had on the same colors. Sam knocked on the door asked was I ready for my night. I told him yes. I felt like Cinderella as he took my hand and walked me to the car. Sam even opened the car door for me. I could not believe it, dinner with Sam, then cocktails. Sam took the long way to the restaurant, which was a very beautiful view of the mountains looking down at the city, and its nightlights were like looking at a picture.

We arrived at the restaurant and there was no one inside, just Sam and I. Sam reserved the restaurant just for me. The table with candles, the lights very dim, soft jazz music playing, and a beautiful vase of roses on the left corner of the table. Sam even pulled my chair out for me. The waiter dressed in a full three-piece suit. The cook had all white on, not a spot on his uniform at all. Sam had already planned our meal, first we had salad with wine, then T-bone steak, baked potato, broccoli, and lemon pound cake for dessert.

During dinner we talked about the lake and how nice it was going to be. We talked about his plans on building a small house behind Bill and Gladys. Bill always called Sam to do all the handiwork on the homes in the neighborhood, so by Sam having a home near all of us it would help everyone. Sam and I chose to not talk about our past relationships, I wanted all new memories, nothing to damper my new happiness. After dinner we went back to my place. Sam walked me to the door and said he would be back, he had to get something out of the car. Sam came back in with a brown bag in his hand and went to the kitchen, got two glasses, and made us martinis.

11 PM

After Sam left, I was ready for bed and very tired, so I took my medications. The martini took my energy, my shower was going to have to wait till morning. I got my PJs and got into bed. As I eased into sleep I thought about my night with Sam and what a wonderful time I had with him. I hoped he'd ask me out again. "Oh, no," I took my medications and had alcohol in my system, Lord help me. The mix of medication and alcohol did make me feel extra good. No wonder some people take their medications with alcohol, it works so much faster and in a good way, well, not a good way but a good way. (I was out like a light.)

The Accident

2 AM

My cell phone was ringing. I sat up in bed, feeling dizzy and confused. Finally, my dizziness went away, and I was able to walk over to the dresser to get my phone. I checked my phone to see who was calling, unknown number. My phone rang again. This time a voice on the other end said, "I told you, you can't hide, if I can't have you no one else can." I yelled back into phone, "Ray, I know it's you, what do you want?" Nothing was said on the other end, just a small laughter, then he hung up. I put my cell phone on the dresser, turned on my bedroom light.

I heard a noise coming from the kitchen. I knew it was Ray. I slipped my blue jeans on, put my cell phone and keys in my back pocket, loaded my gun. I walked towards the kitchen, the back door was opened. I heard a noise in the living room, I eased my way towards the living room, the front door was opened. I walked outside, made my way to the car, got in, and took off.

Soon there was a car behind me. Suddenly bright car lights behind me coming fast. The car got closer and closer and it was Ray. He pulled up beside me and said, "You leave me, we both die!" I drove faster to get away. He drove faster to catch up with me. Soon he caught up with me, rammed his car into mine. Both our cars ran off the side of the road and down a cliff.

I woke up in the hospital with Paul and Linda sitting at my side. The police asked me questions about my night, I told them what happened. The police stated my car was the only car at the scene. I asked them did they check my home. Paul and Linda heard noise at 2 am Paul told the police he saw me get into my car and drive away and didn't see another car. Paul also told the police about Ray.

9 AM

The next morning, Mrs. Waters came to the hospital to visit me. Mrs. Waters said she had talked with the police and they had called Ray's sister and he was with her. There was no way that could be true, I explained to Mrs. Waters I saw him, he talked to me on the phone and then he pulled up to me in the car. I saw his face, heard his voice, just like I was talking to her now. "Please listen to me," I said. Mrs. Waters called the nurse to give me medication and I was asleep.

12 PM

I had slept most of the day away. Very confused about everything that happened and about the things that were told to me. The nurse came in and told me I would be released soon to go home. I didn't want to go back home. Home was not home anymore. Had I gone mad?

When I was discharged, I was taken to the front of the hospital and Paul and Linda were there, waiting on me to take me home. I didn't have much to say, I was too ashamed and unsure of what to say. When I got home, I took my medications early with a glass of wine and went to sleep.

2 AM

I woke up, looked at the clock, it was 2 am I couldn't believe I slept the whole day. I got up, went to the bathroom, then the kitchen. I noticed a shadow, someone sitting in the living room on the chair. I turned on the light. And it was Ray. Ray sitting in my living room with a big smile on his face like this was his home. "Why are you here, Ray? I thought you wanted me out of your life so you could be with your secretary."

"Hi, Rebecca, you couldn't hide from me. I told you I would find you. The noise you heard at night was me. All this time it has been me. Every morning at 2 A.M., it was me. Things can be different if you come back. Things don't have to be this way. Everyone thinks you are losing your mind. You are no good without me, Rebecca. Sam only took you out because he knows you are a lonely, weak person. These people here don't care, they deal with you because Mrs. Waters has told them all about you.

"Just think about how nice it will be to live with me and my secretary, just do your part and take your crazy medication. You need someone to take care of you during this time. You are a mad woman. No man will ever want you, don't miss out on this good deal, Rebecca. Everyone knows your condition and we can take care of you."

As Ray talked and went on and on about how no good I am without him, I fixed my coffee and at the same time reloaded my gun in the kitchen drawer. I even made him a cup of coffee. I took it over to him and his ass was glad to get it. The more he talked, the more I wanted him gone. Next, I pulled my gun on him, shot him in the chest twice. I called 911.

When the police arrived, Ray was dead. The police asked what happened, I gave my story. As I talked Ray's cell phone rang, it was his sister. She told the police he had come to visit me in the hospital and was checking on me. I told the police I hadn't seen him till 2 am sitting in my living room. Then the police stated, "You are one of Mrs. Waters' patients, we are going to have to take you in."

Two months later I was convicted of Ray's death, sentenced to life. I sit every day looking out the window at the institution asylum ward. At 2 am every morning, Ray still haunts me.